SKY ABOVE
EARTH BELOW

Joanna Cotler

A Charlotte Zolotow Book

Harper & Row, Publishers

SKY ABOVE EARTH BELOW
Copyright © 1990 by Joanna Cotler
Printed in the U.S.A. All rights reserved.

Library of Congress Cataloging-in-Publication Data
Cotler, Joanna.
    Sky above earth below / by Joanna Cotler.
        p.   cm.
    "A Charlotte Zolotow book."
    Summary: A little girl notices the patterns and beauty of the sky
and the earth as she sees them through an airplane window.
    ISBN 0-06-021365-5 : $.—ISBN 0-06-021366-3 (lib. bdg.) :
$
    [1. Earth—Fiction.   2. Sky—Fiction.]   I. Title.
PZ7.C8286Sk   1990   89-26743
E—dc20   CIP
                                                              AC

10 9 8 7 6 5 4 3 2 1
First Edition

for Emma

I am traveling through the sky.

Sky above.

Earth below.

Sky above.
Stars shine.

Earth below.
Rivers run.

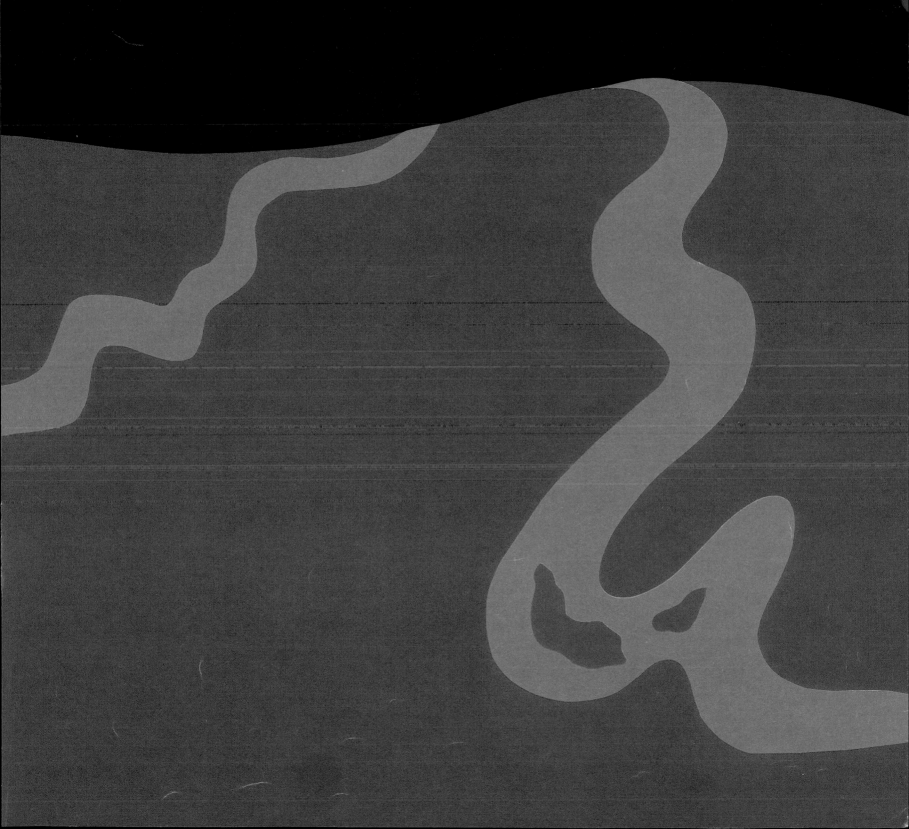

Sky above.
White clouds blanket.

Earth below.
Spiky trees.

Sky above.
Endless space.
Far, far above planets spin.
The night is silent.

Sky above.

Sky forever.

Earth below.
New day begins.
Far, far below
the earth is small.

Mountains are little green hats.

Towns are toys.

Fields are patchwork.

A different place, the earth below.

A different place, the sky above.

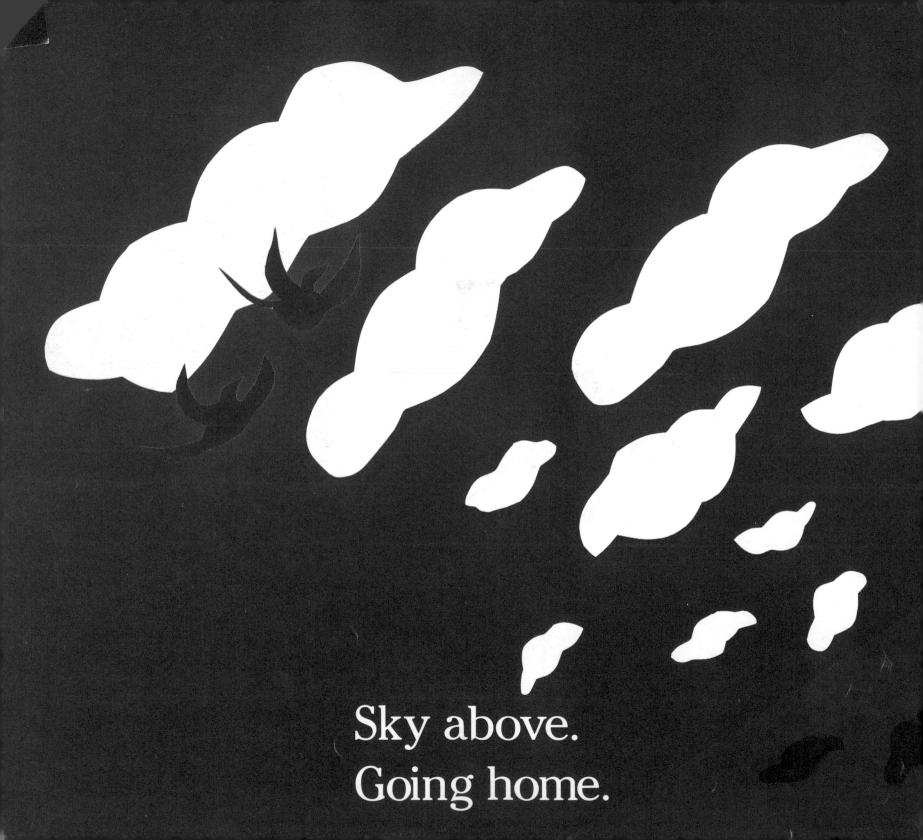

Sky above.
Going home.

Earth below.
Almost there.

Light shines in my window,

light shines for me on my way home.

E
COT

96-01

Cotler, Joanna

Sky Above, Earth Below

QC